Dear Parent:
Your child's love of reading starts here!

Every child learns to read in a different way and at his or her own speed. Some go back and forth between reading levels and read favorite books again and again. Others read through each level in order. You can help your young reader improve and become more confident by encouraging his or her own interests and abilities. From books your child reads with you to the first books he or she reads alone, there are I Can Read Books for every stage of reading:

SHARED READING
Basic language, word repetition, and whimsical illustrations, ideal for sharing with your emergent reader

BEGINNING READING
Short sentences, familiar words, and simple concepts for children eager to read on their own

READING WITH HELP
Engaging stories, longer sentences, and language play for developing readers

READING ALONE
Complex plots, challenging vocabulary, and high-interest topics for the independent reader

I Can Read Books have introduced children to the joy of reading since 1957. Featuring award-winning authors and illustrators and a fabulous cast of beloved characters, I Can Read Books set the standard for beginning readers.

A lifetime of discovery begins with the magical words **"I Can Read!"**

Visit www.icanread.com for information
on enriching your child's reading experience.

For Lacey-Louise Kathleen
—R.S.

I Can Read® and I Can Read Book® are trademarks of HarperCollins Publishers.

Splat the Cat and the Lemonade Stand
Copyright © 2019 by Rob Scotton
All rights reserved. Manufactured in China. No part of this book may be used or reproduced in any manner whatsoever without written permission except in the case of brief quotations embodied in critical articles and reviews. For information address HarperCollins Children's Books, a division of HarperCollins Publishers, 195 Broadway, New York, NY 10007.
www.icanread.com

Library of Congress Control Number: 2018958441
ISBN 978-0-06-269709-7 (trade bdg.)—ISBN 978-0-06-269708-0 (pbk.)

Typography by Rick Farley
19 20 21 22 23 SCP 10 9 8 7 6 5 4 3 2 1 ❖ First Edition

READING 2 WITH HELP

I Can Read!

Splat the Cat

and the Lemonade Stand

Based on the bestselling books by Rob Scotton

Cover art by Rick Farley

by Laura Driscoll

Pictures by Robert Eberz

HARPER

An Imprint of HarperCollinsPublishers

It was the last day of school.

Splat looked at the clock.

Ten minutes to go!

WHAT ARE YOUR
SUMMER PLANS?

Splat could not wait.

He had big, big plans

for the summer.

"I'm going to the new
Super Jumbo Water Park!"
Splat told the class.
"If I can earn money
to pay for half my ticket."

Splat showed Kitten
his list of money-making ideas.
"I'm getting started
after school today," Splat said.
"Ooo, a lemonade stand?" asked Kitten.

"I'll help!" said Spike.

Splat froze.

9

Being partners with Spike
usually didn't go well.
Splat remembered
the science project.

There was the field trip.

And the snow shoveling job.

Just then, the bell rang.

School was out!

"Thanks anyway!"

Splat called to Spike.

"But I think I'll do the stand

on my own!"

At home, Splat filled a box

with everything he needed.

He had lemonade, cups, and a sign.

He was ready!

Splat wheeled it all outside.

At the curb,

Splat stopped in his tracks.

Across the street,

cats were lined up

at a different lemonade stand.

"Hi, Splat!" Spike called out

from behind the table.

Splat fumed.

But Splat did not want Spike

to see he was upset.

So Splat set up

his lemonade stand.

He made a change to his sign.

Cats began coming over.

"It's working!" Splat said.

SUPER SWEET
Lemonade
25 cents

Just then, Spike's dad

got home from work.

"Need some ice, son?" he asked Spike.

"Thanks, Dad!" Spike replied.

Spike made a change to his sign.
Cats began moving back
to Spike's stand.

ICE COLD LEMONADE 25¢

Splat lowered his price.

Spike did, too.

SUPER SWEET
Lemonade
10 ~~20~~ cents

Splat offered two cups
for the price of one.

SUPER SWEET
Lemonade
2 for 10 ~~25~~ cents

Spike offered three.

ICE COLD
LEMONADE
~~25¢~~ 10¢ for 3 cups

And now Spike had music, too!

It was like a party

over at Spike's stand!

Splat had to do something.

All those cats

couldn't even see his sign!

So Splat ran inside
to get some things.
"I have to get my sign up higher,"
Splat said.

SUPER SWEET
Lemonade
2 for 10 ~~25~~ cents

"Higher!"

"Higher!"

Splat crashed into Spike's table.

Spike's lemonade spilled everywhere.

"Sorry, Spike," Splat said.

Spike looked mad.

Splat didn't blame him.

"Want to help me

with my lemonade stand?"

Splat asked.

Spike grinned.

"Sure!" he replied.

So Splat and Spike worked together.

They had lots of customers.

Soon they sold out of lemonade.

The cash box was full.

"Nice working with you, Spike!"
Splat said.

And he meant it.

"You too," said Spike.
"Super Jumbo Water Park,
here we come!"